Titles in Papercuts:

QUEEN OF FLIES
TIM COLLINS

SCISSOR MAN
TIM COLLINS

SIGNAL
TIM COLLINS

WAXWORK
TIM COLLINS

PEACE
STEPH CROWLEY

THAW
STEPH CROWLEY

A LITTLE SECRET
ANN EVANS

VIRAL
ANN EVANS

DARK TIDE
JON MAYHEW

THE LANE
IAIN MCLAUGHLIN

BIOLOGY
EMMA NORRY

WILD
EMMA NORRY

MIRRORS
KATE ORMAND

ONE WAY
KATE ORMAND

THE TRICK
KATE ORMAND

ALICE
DANNY PEARSON

THE SICKNESS
JACQUELINE RAYNER

WANTED
JENNI SPANGLER

Badger Publishing Limited, Oldmedow Road, Hardwick Industrial Estate, King's Lynn PE30 4JJ

Telephone: 01438 791037

www.badgerlearning.co.uk

THAW

STEPH CROWLEY | JAMES LAWRENCE

'Which was worse? Him being dead, or him still being alive?'

Thaw ISBN 978-1-78837-524-5

Text © Steph Crowley 2020
Complete work © Badger Publishing Limited 2020

Publisher / Senior Editor: Danny Pearson
Editor: Claire Wood
Copyeditor: Cheryl Lanyon
Designer: Bigtop Design Ltd
Illustration: James Lawrence

2 4 6 8 10 9 7 5 3 1

CHAPTER 1
MINUS SEVEN

Taylor was glad of her snowsuit, even though it felt like wearing a sleeping bag. She sat in the helicopter next to Miles, waiting for lift off.

"Nice warm day." Their pilot Viktor's breath was a cloud of white steam.

"Yes," said Rosa. "Minus seven."

Taylor couldn't tell if they were joking. The landing pad was sheltered by snow-covered hills, and behind them the sea was sparkling blue and icy. Perhaps Viktor and Rosa were used to it.

"Headsets on," said Viktor. "Here we go."

Viktor started the engine. Taylor put the bulky headphones on her head. It was still loud. She took a few slow, deep breaths to calm her nervous stomach. The flight here in the tiny twelve-seater plane had been scary enough.

Miles snapped photos as they gradually rose into the sky. "This is amazing!" he shouted over the din.

Taylor braved a peek out of the window. They were so high. The town of King's Bay shrank until it looked like a set of children's building blocks, scattered across the snow. She was in the furthest corner of the world, and she was in a helicopter. A helicopter! On her way to a real research base to do real, important science. Miles was right. It was amazing.

And terrifying.

"You're not used to much snow in the UK," said Viktor, his voice clear through the headphones.

"Are you from here?" asked Taylor. "From Norway, I mean, not right here."

No one could be from here. Only scientists and adventurers would come this far into the Arctic.

"Iceland," said Viktor.

"And I'm from Mexico." Rosa grinned. "This weather was a big change!"

"We're an international team," said Viktor. "Miguel is from Mexico too. Simon, the geologist, is from Austria. Our medical doctor, Louise, is American."

"Tell me about your programme," said Rosa. "You are 'bright sparks', yes? Scientists of tomorrow."

Miles perked up at this. "Yes. I passed my chemistry A-level when I was 14. I'm working on university-level courses now."

Taylor tried not to roll her eyes. Miles had gone on about his 'incredible' exam results for the whole flight to Norway. Blah blah blah, doing algebra before he was potty-trained, or whatever.

"There are only twenty places in STEMvision, so they only take the best." Miles scanned Taylor from head to foot. "That's the idea, anyway."

Rude. Maybe Taylor didn't take her GCSEs in the womb, like Miles. She'd struggled at school for years — especially at tests — until someone noticed she was dyslexic.

She had a lot of catching up to do. But she had a real knack for science. The ideas and explanations made perfect sense to her. It was the physics teacher who told her about STEMvision and helped her apply. The scheme sent teenagers all over the world to take part in real research projects.

There was a jolt. The helicopter swayed to the side then dropped several feet. Taylor's breakfast threatened to appear again.

"Only turbulence," said Rosa. "The wind is wild here."

Taylor smiled and pretended she was totally cool with it. Definitely not about to wet herself from fear.

Miles still wasn't done. "Mine was the number one application, actually. My essay on genetic testing —"

The helicopter swung violently to the side. Taylor banged into Miles's shoulder. He frowned.

"This is a mild day," said Viktor. "I've been on worse flights."

"We only take the helicopter in good weather. Sometimes we wait several days for good conditions," said Rosa. "We're expecting a storm tomorrow, and no one will come in or out of the base until it passes."

Right on cue, the helicopter began to shudder. Taylor closed her eyes and counted her breath — in, two, three, four; out, two, three, four.

"There's the base," said Rosa.

Greyish shapes appeared on the horizon and quickly grew closer. The base was smaller than Taylor had expected. Pods sat on thick stilts side-by-side in the snow. They were like tubes cut in half longways. Rows of solar panels on the roofs gleamed in the sun.

"Hang on!" said Viktor. "It might be a bumpy landing."

*

Solid ground at last. They climbed out and entered a tunnel — Pod B. The first room was the boot room, where they stored all their outside gear. Taylor was pleasantly surprised at how warm the place was. They were given a quick tour, leaving their cases by the door.

"Pod B is our living area," said Rosa. "It's home. Boot room, living room and, at the back, storage for food, mostly."

There were three worn sofas around a low coffee table. A dining table and eight yellow, plastic chairs stood in the centre of the room. Beyond that was a small kitchen.

"It looks so normal," said Taylor. It was like the staffroom at her mum's office.

Miles scoffed. "What did you expect?"

Taylor ignored him.

"Pod A is our lab. We'll show you everything tomorrow. And Pod C has the sleeping quarters and the radio room, where we can contact King's Bay in case of an emergency," Rosa said. "Bring your bags, I'll show Taylor her bunk. Viktor, you can take Miles."

The room wasn't much bigger than Taylor's bedroom at home. It had three sets of bunk beds and a row of thin cabinets, like school lockers. The door had a small window which looked out into the corridor, but there were no skylights here. With the lights off, it would be completely dark.

"You can have any bed on this side," said Rosa.

Taylor heaved her wheelie case onto the nearest bed and sat down. She was exhausted after travelling all day.

"Your friend has a lot to say." Rosa raised her eyebrows.

"He's not my friend," said Taylor. "We were paired up by STEMvision. They send two people to each project."

"What other projects are there?"

"Studying volcanoes in Hawaii. Two girls went to South America to help build this giant telescope. There was one about lemurs…"

"And you picked the Arctic?" Rosa laughed.

"We didn't get to choose." Wait, that sounded ungrateful. "I mean, not that I don't like it here, it's a great opportunity…"

"Ha! It's fine. You would have picked somewhere warmer, right?"

"Maybe." Taylor smiled. "But then I wouldn't get to be with wonderful Miles, who is of course absolutely perfect in every single way."

Rosa laughed again. "Don't worry, people like him are all talk. Harmless."

Taylor hesitated. "I was worried no one would speak English. I tried to learn Norwegian from an app, but it wouldn't stick. All I remember is 'bjørnen spiser meg'."

"The bear is eating me! Let's hope you don't need to use it!" laughed Rosa.

Taylor smoothed out the blankets. Suddenly she felt shy and awkward. She'd been so excited about this trip. What if she wasn't good enough after all, and they were expecting someone much smarter? "Thank you for having me," she blurted out.

"You're so welcome," said Rosa. "And you came at the perfect time. We've had a fantastic breakthrough. Miguel and I have been studying lifeforms trapped in the ice for thousands of years. And now that the ice is thawing, some of them are coming back to life."

CHAPTER 2
BLOOD

Taylor woke in complete darkness. She reached for her bedside lamp and bumped into the wall — which is when she remembered she was at the research base. A thrill ran right down to her toes. She fumbled around for her phone. No service. But at least she could check the time: 7.14am.

Miles was already awake. He was at the kitchen table, droning on about how he'd taken most of his exams early.

"It gave me more time to work on my music. I don't suppose you play an instrument, Taylor?" he asked, with a smug look of I'm-better-than-you.

"Grade eight piano and oboe." Total lie. But worth it to watch his face fall. Anyway, he couldn't prove her wrong. She was sick of his bragging. He'd spent most of last night talking about himself, when Taylor had wanted to ask the scientists about their work. "What's the plan for today?" she asked the group.

"Miguel and Simon have brought another set of ice core samples," said Rosa. "Sorry we didn't wake you to go with them. They had to leave early, to miss the storm. Shall we go through?"

"Ready when you are." Miles put his book down.

"This way," said Rosa.

It was exciting to be inside a real lab. Laptops and microscopes dotted the benches. One wall had a row of upright fridges full of test tubes. Another wall was lined with large, grey machinery which Taylor didn't recognize.

Miles swaggered over to the door marked Ice Core Processing.

"You need to suit up before you go in there." Rosa pointed to a row of white plastic overalls hanging from hooks.

Miles rolled his eyes but did what she said. There was a slight twitch at the corner of Rosa's mouth. He was starting to annoy her.

"Should I put one on?" asked Taylor.

"Why don't I show you the nematode worms first? We don't need suits for those."

Miles zipped the suit and slid on blue latex gloves.

"Hairnets are in the box," Rosa called out.

"I'm not wearing a hairnet," said Miles.

"Then you're not going in."

He sighed and grabbed a hairnet from the box.

"It's a nice look on you," said Taylor. "Like a school dinner-lady."

Miles headed into the ice core room. Rosa pulled up two stools and brought over a petri dish. She put it under the microscope.

"This is Barbara." Rosa switched on a monitor and the image from the microscope appeared. She adjusted the focus and a thin, see-through worm wriggled on the screen. "We think she is over 40,000 years old."

"How did she survive in the ice?"

"She was —"

A crash from the ice core room cut her off. They jumped to their feet.

"Everyone OK?" Rosa called out.

"Fine. Ow! Fine." Simon came through the doorway clasping his wrist. "I dropped a collection tube and cut my hand on the glass. It went right through the glove."

Miguel and Miles came through behind him. Miles was white as a sheet. It seemed Mr Amazing couldn't deal with the sight of blood.

"It ruined the sample," Simon said. "What a waste."

"Accidents happen," said Miguel. "Miles, look after him while I find the doc."

"I don't think…" Miles looked like he would vomit or faint, or both. Blood dripped from Simon's arm.

"I'll sit with him," said Taylor. "Miles can get the doctor."

"I'll clear up," said Miguel.

"Need help?" asked Rosa.

"No, it'll only take five minutes," replied Miguel.

Taylor held the door open for Simon and pulled out the nearest chair.

CONTROLLED
ENVIRONMENT

"Thanks. The blood makes it look worse than it is." Simon had been pale to begin with, but he was starting to look grey. It probably hurt more than he was admitting.

Louise, the doctor, rushed in from Pod C and went straight to Simon. "Show me, show me. Oh dear! There's nothing stuck in there. I'll patch you up in no time."

An hour later, everything was sorted. The team spent the morning taking readings from the undamaged ice cores: measuring layers and taking samples of the air in the bubbles. Miles and Taylor were asked to collect results from the various machines and put them into the computer.

"It's a bit basic, isn't it?" whispered Miles as they sat side-by-side. "Typing. Spreadsheets. Boring."

Taylor didn't think it was boring. She carefully checked everything, scared she would write the letters the wrong way around and spoil the whole experiment.

"When do you think they'll let us do the good stuff?" asked Miles.

Taylor shrugged and kept typing.

"They use snowmobiles to collect the samples. Can you ride one? I can."

"Of course you can," said Taylor.

Miles shuffled closer. "Don't be like that. I'm sorry, OK? I know I can be…"

"A jerk?"

"I was going to say 'superior'. People always say I act superior. I don't mean to be. It's hard to talk to normal people sometimes, because I'm so clever."

Taylor stopped typing and glared at him.

"That didn't come out right. You're clever too. We should be friends," said Miles.

She didn't bother to answer. It was going to be a long two weeks, stuck indoors with him. At least the scientists were all friendly. And that was why she was here, after all.

"Thanks, by the way," said Miles.

"For what?" asked Taylor

"Not laughing at me. I don't like blood. I was meant to go to the cancer research centre, but when I found out they dealt with blood and tissue samples, I asked to switch. That's why I'm here."

"You should be grateful then," snapped Taylor. "Try to be nicer."

"Right," said Miles. "Nicer."

CHAPTER 3
INFECTED

Day two on the base and Taylor woke at 5am. Rosa was still snoring so Taylor shuffled out in her pyjamas without turning on the lights. In the living area, Louise, Viktor and Miguel were talking in hushed tones. They stopped suddenly when they noticed Taylor.

"You're up early," said Louise.

"I think my body clock is a bit confused."

"That can happen." Miguel stood up and went into the kitchen. "You're in time for the first pot of coffee, anyway."

"Thanks," said Taylor.

"We should radio for a lift," said Louise.
Viktor nodded.

"What's wrong?" asked Taylor.

"Simon isn't well. His hand might be infected."
She rubbed her forehead.

"There's no visibility at all today. Blizzard
conditions. We won't get a helicopter through
this," said Miguel.

"It's not an emergency yet. But I'd feel better
knowing someone is on standby, just in case.
He won't be able to ride a snowmobile to town,"
replied Louise.

"You're right." Miguel drained his coffee.
"I'll do it."

He headed out towards the radio room.

"Should we be worried?" asked Taylor.

"No. If we were at home I wouldn't be concerned at all, but we play things ultra-safe here." Louise stood up and put her cup in the sink. "I'm going to see if his temperature has come down."

Taylor poured coffee and listened to the sounds of the wind. Miles came in as she was washing up.

"Did you hear about Simon?" asked Taylor.

"He was awake half the night moaning." Miles yawned.

"They're calling a helicopter. But it won't be today, because of the storm."

"Scary," said Miles. "They're flying him out for a little cut because, if he gets worse, they won't be able to get help in time. Doesn't it worry you?"

"I suppose…" She hadn't really thought about it until now. "It's good to be careful."

"That's what the medical forms were for. Remember? The huge tick list: have you ever had heart problems, allergies, asthma..."

"Everyone filled those out. It's a standard thing," snapped Taylor.

"If you have a fit or something, you'll be dead before they get you to a hospital." His eyes were wide. He scratched the back of his head and stared into space.

"Cheerful," replied Taylor. Smug, show-off Miles was more fun than doom-and-gloom Miles.

"Sorry." He sat down. "I get anxious about health stuff. I wasn't worried until the doctor came into our room every hour checking Simon's temperature. It seems extreme for an infected cut."

"I wouldn't know." She poured him a coffee and placed it on the table beside him.

"And he's got this rash on his arm. Raised red lines. It looks like his blood vessels are trying to escape through his skin. That's not just an infection, right?"

"I don't know, Miles, that's what the doctor is for!" Taylor paused; took a breath. "You're stressing over nothing."

"The doctor doesn't know either," he replied.

*

Simon slept for most of the day.

The others kept Taylor and Miles busy, teaching them how to use the equipment. It was fascinating, and Taylor didn't even mind missing out on the beaches of Hawaii. The most interesting things were the worms which had survived centuries in the ice. If they could find a way to freeze human lives like that, people could travel all over the universe in a single lifetime.

Working seemed to keep everyone's minds off Simon's injury. This was good, since the helicopter wouldn't arrive for at least 24 hours.

By the evening Simon had got up from his bunk, but he was a mess. He shook and coughed, slurring his words. Taylor saw the rash, starting beneath the bandage and stretching up his arm.

Louise put him back in bed.

"I have no idea what's causing the rash," she said. "I've never seen anything like it."

They tried to keep busy in the evening. Taylor played cards with Rosa and Louise. Miles was reading, and Viktor wrote a report on his laptop. Miguel entered the room looking worried.

"Hey, doc?"

Louise put down her cards.

"Infected wounds aren't contagious, right?" asked Miguel.

Miles flinched.

"Not unless you put your broken skin against his," said Louise.

"It's probably nothing but in the shower I noticed this. It's just a bruise, right?" He tugged the collar of his shirt. Where his shoulder met his neck were the same bulging, red lines which Simon had on his arm.

Silence fell across the room as all eyes fixed on Miguel's neck.

"Anything else?" asked Louise. "Any coughing or dizziness?" Her tone had completely changed. She was calm, but there was a seriousness which felt different from earlier.

"I'm not sure," said Miguel, his eyes darting from one person to the next. Everyone waited for his answer. "Maybe I was a little dizzy in the shower, but I skipped lunch so I thought…"

"Take a seat. I'm sure it's nothing," said Louise, but her tone was serious. She grabbed the first-aid kit from beneath the sink. "I'm going to take your temperature."

Nobody spoke as she clicked the thermometer together and pointed it into his ear. It bleeped.

"38.6 degrees Celsius." She frowned. "If you have the same symptoms as Simon, it might have nothing to do with the cut."

"So he's caught some regular bug from outside the base," said Rosa.

"I haven't been off the base for two months. Neither has Simon," said Miguel.

"Only Viktor and I have been off-base recently," said Rosa. "And the kids."

Everyone's gaze now shifted to Taylor and Miles.

"Well it's not me!" snapped Miles. "There's nothing wrong with me."

"Have either of you noticed any symptoms? Anything at all?" asked Louise. "Either today or before you arrived here? Have you been sick?"

Taylor shook her head. Louise unclipped the top of the thermometer and took a new one from a sterile packet. "I'm going to take your temperatures."

"I don't want to!" said Miles, voice full of fear.

"Hey," said Taylor, "it's OK. If you don't check, you'll worry all night, right?"

He agreed, and Louise did her job. Both teenagers had temperatures in the normal range.

"So if they didn't bring it in from the outside —" started Louise, "where does that leave us?"

"The core sample," said Rosa. "Miguel and Simon were both in the room when the glass broke. It could be airborne."

Miles went white. He had been in the room too. "I need to go home. We don't have to be here, we're kids. You have to get us out of here." He stood up, as if he could run home.

"We've called the helicopter," said Louise. "Until it can fly, we need to sit tight and stay calm. Miguel, take some tablets to control your fever and go to bed."

They decided Miles and Viktor should sleep in the living room, leaving their sleeping quarters to the sick men. Rosa returned to the radio to update King's Bay. Louise took swabs from Simon and Miguel and hurried into the lab to see if she could find the cause of the illness.

Miles and Taylor played a few games of rummy — the only card game they both knew. Miles kept looking around nervously, as if someone might sneak up on him. Twice he left the table to wash his hands.

"What did you write your application essay on?" Taylor asked after a while. Anything to get his mind off obsessing about the illness. All his swagger had been wiped away.

To her surprise, she found herself interested in his ideas and what he had to say. "You know," she said, after a long discussion, "you're pretty interesting, when you stop talking about yourself for five minutes."

CHAPTER 4
SIMON

"Louise! Doc! Louise!"

The yelling startled Taylor awake, her heart pounding. Louise raced out from the lab and straight across the living room towards the sleeping quarters.

Taylor must have nodded off in the living room. Miles lay on the sofa opposite.

Moments later they heard shouting, banging, crashing. A woman screamed. Taylor was frozen to the spot. Should she be running to help, or running away? A yell — no, more like a roar. Then silence.

"I want to go home," moaned Miles. "I should have gone to cancer research. I wasn't meant to be here."

It seemed like forever as they waited. Taylor made coffee. It was the only thing she could think of. Miles sat on the sofa, knees to his chest, and said nothing.

After what seemed an age, Louise and Rosa walked into the living room.

"Is Simon OK?" asked Miles, jumping to his feet.

"No. No he isn't," said Rosa.

"I'm afraid Simon has passed away," said Louise.

"The shouting…?" asked Taylor.

"It wasn't like him," said Rosa. "Simon was so gentle, what could make him lash out like that?"

"Did he hurt you?" asked Louise.

Rosa shook her head.

"It wasn't him. It was the disease," said Louise. "It made him aggressive. He couldn't help it."

Taylor gripped the edge of the sink. She felt like the air had been knocked out of her. How was this possible? He had been fine when they arrived.

"You've got to get us out of here," said Miles. "Now!"

"Not an option," said Rosa. "It's too dangerous in this storm."

"What about Miguel?" asked Taylor.

"Miguel is sleeping," said Louise. "But he has gone downhill. We need to seriously consider what to do next. First, we need to radio in to base. Then we wrap the body…"

"Oh God," said Taylor. The body. Simon was a man and now he was a body.

They wrapped Simon's body in blankets and carried it into the storage room. Miles and Taylor tried not to look.

"We're all going to catch this — whatever it is," said Miles.

"Shut up, OK? You're not helping," snapped Taylor. She wanted to text her mum, but there was no reception, as always.

"I could steal a snowmobile," said Miles.

"You'll die on the ice," replied Taylor.

"Die on the ice or die here."

"You're too smart to risk it."

Miles grunted.

They gathered round the table — Taylor, Miles and the three scientists who were left. The mood was bleak.

"The flight crew are saying 16 hours," said Viktor. "We can be in King's Bay by dinner time tomorrow. We're first priority. It will take two trips."

Sixteen hours. Not long. They could manage.

"Miguel will go on the first flight, so he can get hospital treatment," said Rosa.

"No," said Miles. "Get the healthy people out first. For all we know, Miguel is going to die anyway."

"Don't be so selfish," said Rosa.

"Actually, he might be right," said Louise. She ran her hand through her hair, her expression tense. "I've been looking at the samples in the lab. Whatever this is, it came from the ice. It's a virus. Something humans no longer have any immunity to. That's why it killed Simon so quickly."

"Will Miguel die too?" asked Taylor.

"I don't know." Louise shook her head. "We don't know how it spreads, but it's fast and dangerous. We need to think. It might be safest if the virus never leaves this base."

"Leave Miguel here?" asked Rosa.

It was warm in the pod but Taylor's blood ran ice cold.

"If I'm right, this virus is something we haven't seen before. We have to keep it from spreading," Louise sighed. "We might need to make some hard choices."

"What do you mean?" asked Miles. "Say what you mean." From across the table, Taylor could see he was shaking.

"It's possible we've all been exposed. We eat together, sleep together, we've all been in and out of the lab." She folded her arms. "I think everyone should go to bed and get some sleep. If the helicopter comes tomorrow, we'll need our energy for the journey."

"If?" said Viktor.

"If any of us are showing symptoms in the morning, we seal the base and cancel the helicopter," replied Louise.

"So we can all catch the virus?" asked Viktor.

"Do you want to take this home to your family? This could spread, worse than Ebola," said Louise.

"The children…" Rosa whispered. "We can't do this to them."

"I hope we won't have to." Louise stood up. "But I'm in charge of this mission. I have a duty to make the right call."

Miles was strangely quiet. Taylor expected him to start shouting, but instead he stared into the middle distance and nodded along with them. What was he thinking? His nightmare scenario had come true.

"I'm going back into the lab," said Louise.

"I'm coming with you," said Rosa. "I'll help any way I can."

"Us too," said Taylor, but Louise shook her head.

"Please, try to sleep."

The door to the lab closed behind them.

"I wasn't meant to be here," whispered Miles.

CHAPTER 5
MIGUEL

It was morning when the shouting started again.

Miguel had woken, and found himself locked in the bedroom. His shouts went from English to Spanish as he banged his fists on the door, begging to be let out. He was better and the fever had gone away, he said. But they recognized the aggression in his voice — like with Simon.

"What if he's right?" asked Taylor. "Shouldn't we check?"

"No!" Miles was wide-eyed. "Open the door and we're all infected. You saw what happened to Simon. It's too late for him."

"How can you be so cold?" asked Taylor.

"I left him with food and water," said Louise. "If he is getting better, he will be safe until help arrives. If he isn't…"

"Letting him out won't help," finished Rosa.

The pounding of fists stopped and was replaced by a slower, louder, slamming noise. Bang. Bang. Bang.

"He's trying to break the door down," said Miles.

"He won't get through," said Louise.

"I hope he doesn't hurt himself," said Rosa.

"Rosa," said Viktor quietly, "your arm."

Red lines on her hand ran up her arm. She pulled back her sleeve and, sure enough, there was the tell-tale spider web of raised, red veins.

Bang.

"Oh." Rosa sank into a chair. "Oh no!"

"Rosa wasn't there when the glass broke." Viktor said what everyone was thinking. "That's proof, isn't it? It's contagious."

Bang.

"We have to leave now!" shouted Miles.

"The helicopter will be here in a few hours," said Viktor.

"We should take the snowmobiles," Miles insisted.

"It's too dangerous," said Viktor.

Bang.

"Nobody leaves," said Louise. The others fell silent and looked to her. "We can't risk taking the disease with us. If something like this gets out in a city…"

Bang.

"You can't do this to us," said Miles.

"We'll stay separate from the infected people. In 48 hours we'll know. We can call the helicopter later, when we can be sure we're not infected," replied Louise.

"When Miguel and I are dead," said Rosa.

"Rosa," said Louise, "I'm so sorry. It might not come to that. I'm going to do everything I can to —"

"Stop. It's OK. It's not your fault." Rosa walked towards the sleeping quarters. "You need to lock me up. For everyone's safety."

Taylor looked around helplessly. What could she do to help? She felt like this was a private moment. These people had lived and worked together for months. Taylor and Miles were strangers, crashing someone's funeral and helping themselves to the buffet. It was wrong, somehow, to witness this conversation.

"Listen," said Viktor. "Listen! The banging has stopped."

They peered in at Miguel through the little, round window. He lay slumped on the floor, face-down.

"Is he…?" Taylor couldn't bring herself to finish the sentence.

"We can't open the door to check," said Louise.

"But if he's not dead, if he needs help…" Taylor protested.

"We can't risk it," said Louise.

For the first time, Taylor cried. The tears started falling, silently, as they shuffled out of the sleeping pod and into the main room.

She knew Louise was trying to keep them alive, but this was too cruel.

*

Fifteen minutes later there was a shout from the radio room. They all rushed in. Taylor turned her face away as they passed the sleeping quarters, not wanting to see whether Miguel had moved. Which was worse? Him being dead, or him still being alive?

The radio room was trashed. The speaker was smashed, the microphone cord slashed in several places, everything snipped and twisted and ruined.

"Who did this?" demanded Louise. "Which one of you did this?" There was fury in her voice. "You think it means that I can't now cancel the helicopter, but it makes no difference. I will turn them away. All you've done is made things harder for us."

Taylor was shaking. She was frightened and felt guilty, even though she hadn't done it. She wanted the helicopter to come and get her, no matter what. She was hoping for it.

They all stared at each other. Someone had destroyed their only line of communication. Louise was trying to make decisions for the good of everyone, but someone here was only looking out for themselves.

"It was probably Miguel. You saw how violent he was," said Miles.

"Miguel has been locked in his room," said Viktor.

"Rosa, then!" said Miles. "She might have known she was sick for hours before we saw the marks on her arm. She could have done this to try to escape."

"Rosa put herself in quarantine," said Viktor. "Why would she do something like this?"

"Because the virus makes people violent," said Miles.

Viktor stared at him: a long, steady glare. He obviously thought Miles had done it. Taylor feared he was right.

The base felt ten times smaller than the night they'd arrived. Were there clouds of virus washing over them, even now?

They returned to the lab, though no one's heart was in it. The ice core samples had been left to melt, ruined. They sealed the boxes the ice samples were in, though it was probably a waste of time. Still, it felt better to do something, no matter how hopeless.

Only Louise worked with passion, desperate to find out anything she could about the virus.

Taylor watched the clock ticking. She wanted to go home. Why couldn't she have gone to Hawaii?

Four o'clock. An hour before the helicopter was due to arrive.

"I've got something," said Louise, standing so suddenly her stool tipped over and clattered against the hard floor.

"A cure?" asked Miles.

"No. But a test. I can test to see if we're infected."

Taylor's stomach somersaulted. Did she even want to know?

"First, I need everyone's agreement. If we test positive, we stay behind. We can't risk releasing this into the world. Anyone who tests negative can get on the helicopter. I'll ask them to return with hazard suits and medication for the people left behind."

"Agreed," said Victor.

"OK," said Taylor.

Miles nodded.

Louise filled four small bottles with a pale-blueish liquid and stuck a barcode label onto each one. She scanned them into her computer one at a time and typed their names beside the codes. Four names. Four survivors. So far.

"We'll need a sample of each person's saliva," she explained, as she handed out cotton buds. "Swipe it around the inside of your cheek."

They did as they were told. Louise placed each one in turn into a labelled bottle and swirled it around, before sealing the lid.

She slotted the bottles into a machine which was linked to her laptop. "It will take thirty minutes," she said. "Pack up, I don't want the helicopter crew waiting."

They began packing up the lab. Either everyone would be gone soon, or the remaining people would be too ill to continue the work. Notes had to be backed up, machinery shut down, refrigeration units cleared. Someone else would

have to pick up the rest of the equipment —
eventually. Taylor carried things backwards and
forwards and tried not to think. She worked like a
zombie, moving and talking but barely aware of
what she was doing.

Until the machine bleeped to say the results
were ready.

They stood around the machine. Louise's hands
trembled as she opened the results.

Taylor leaned in to see, but it was a jumble of
numbers and letters.

Louise sighed. "I'm infected." She took Viktor's
hand. "And so are you."

Viktor bit his lip, closed his eyes, nodded.

"What about me?" asked Miles.

"You're OK. Negative. Both of you are negative."

Taylor was nearly sick. Relief, immediately
followed by guilt.

"I'm happy for you." Louise closed the laptop. "I couldn't forgive myself if something happened to the two of you."

"Go," said Viktor. "Get your things, go into the snowsuit room. Quickly."

"Here." Louise handed Taylor a thumb drive. "Give it to the medical staff in King's Bay. It's everything I've learned about the virus. It'll give them the best chance of helping us. And this." She handed them a folded sheet of paper. "It's a letter, explaining why they must not come inside."

"I'm sorry," said Taylor.

"Go!" said Louise.

CHAPTER 6
HOME

Taylor dragged her wheelie case out into the snow. She had probably forgotten something. She didn't care. She didn't care about any of it. She'd had to shut the door behind them. Shut the door on Louise and Viktor and Rosa. At least she wouldn't be around when the rage kicked in.

The helicopter took off. She didn't care about turbulence this time. From the sky the base looked smaller and smaller — grey lumps on a white landscape, like tombstones.

Taylor tried to explain to the pilot. She spoke about the accident, the first symptoms, and how they tried to help Simon and Miguel. How the men became so violent.

She told them how hard, Louise, the doctor worked to save them, and how brave and noble the scientists had been at the end. They were heroes, and people should know. She hoped they would get help in time, but it seemed unlikely. Sometimes she had to stop talking because she was crying too hard.

Miles stared out of the window. Perhaps he was in shock.

At the end of the flight they were helped down from the helicopter and bundled into an office full of people. Arrangements had already been made to return them home. They were brought hot drinks. Taylor handed over the thumb drive.

"We made it out," she said to Miles, as they sipped cocoa and waited for transport.

"We made it out," said Miles.

Wait.

"Miles. Your neck."

The spidery raised lines were poking out from the top of his coat. He pulled up his hood.

"Miles. The marks — the marks on your neck!" Taylor leapt out of her chair. "It was… the test was wrong."

"She shouldn't have left the machine while she packed," said Miles.

Oh no. He'd cheated. "But it… how?" Taylor spluttered.

"First, I turned down the sensitivity, but it was still positive. So I swapped my barcode with Louise's."

"What!" Taylor backed away from him. "You… how could… you've put everyone in danger. And Louise wasn't ill… how could you do this to her?"

"She would have left us there to die," said Miles. "We'll get help now. I did the right thing."

"But the virus," Taylor cried out. "It's going to spread. More people are going to die!"

Miles shrugged his shoulders. The spidery lines were climbing up his neck. "No time to waste then. They'd best get started on that cure."

THE END

ABOUT THE AUTHOR

Steph Crowley lives on top of a hill in Staffordshire where it's always foggy.

When she isn't writing, she can usually be found doing community drama projects, sipping herbal tea or operating heavy machinery.

Her ambition is one day to be the oldest person alive (which still won't be enough time to turn all her ideas into books).

ABOUT THE ARTIST

James Lawrence hails from a faraway land of Vikings and motorcycles. He spends his days drawing rad pictures and chugging iced tea.

He is the creator of the fantasy wrestling webcomic The Legend of La Mariposa.